T0159134

Coming Back From Nowhere

Abigail Westby & Julie Weeber

authorHOUSE®

AuthorHouse™
1663 Liberty Drive
Bloomington, IN 47403
www.authorhouse.com
Phone: 1-800-839-8640

First published by AuthorHouse 12/20/2011

ISBN: 978-1-4634-0240-2 (ebk)
ISBN: 978-1-4634-0242-6 (sc)

Library of Congress Control Number: 2011907926

Printed in the United States of America

Table of Contents:

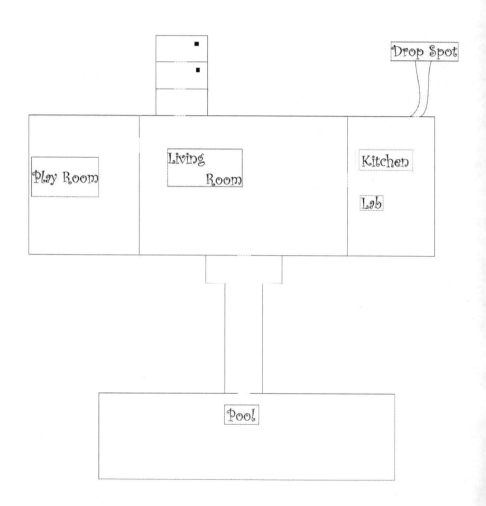

Drop Spot

Play Room

Living Room

Kitchen

Lab

Pool

Chapter 1

The Pool

Ah! School is finally over! You look forward to an enjoyable summer, catching some sun at the lake, going to your favorite amusement parks, you know, the usual. Unfortunately, chores are included in that, but you refuse to let that get the better of you. You can't wait to do all the fun summer things with your best friend, especially going swimming at the college pool. Looking back, you thought it would be a normal summer, you never knew how wrong a person could be!

It all started the day your mom had promised to take you and your friend swimming at the college pool. You both loved that pool because it was actually two pools. One is a lap pool but the other one is a diving pool 12-14 feet deep. That one is your favorite.

Before even getting into the pool, both of you have to do your traditional get-over-the-jitters dives. After you do yours and are waiting for your friend to finish theirs, you go down and try to touch the bottom. Down you go, 3 feet...6 feet... 9 and then 12 feet. You're on the bottom feeling good, you have lots of air and you like the way the pressure feels on your ears, after you pop them.

You float along the bottom, using the wall for guidance. You get to a certain part in the wall and it seems to give way! At first your mind won't accept what just happened. You think that you hit a dent in the wall, but even as your turn your head to look, you know that's not what happened. All you see is the shocking sight of your wrist sticking out of the wall! You jerk your hand out and lose all your preciously stored air.

A million things are speeding through your head as you shoot to the surface. When you get there, you look around for your friend who happens to be swimming towards you. You realize that a look of terror must be on your face because your friend's smile quickly turns to a look of concern.

"What's the matter?" they ask.

After a few unsuccessful tries you take a deep breath and try to calm down. Eventually you are able to tell them what happened. You get the expected reaction, they don't quite believe you.

"Come on, that stuff only happens in sci-fi!"

"Look," you say, "something happened down there. I saw it with my own eyes and even I don't believe it! If I can find that spot again will you believe me?"

Your friend agrees to go down with you. So down you go

2

again, 3 feet, 6... 9... and 12 feet. You go to where you think it might be. You stay down there for awhile, trying to find the surreal place in the wall again. You're just about to give up and go back to the surface for a breath when, behind you, your friend yells and loses all of their air. When you turn around you get a view of their feet as they shoot to the surface. When you join them, their face mirrors what yours must have looked like. Your friend says, with almost panic in their voice, "I... did you see that??!! ... My hand... it was gone!!"

You say, "See!! I told you it was for real!"

"I saw it but I don't believe it!"

There is a pause as both of you think about what happened, and try to figure out what to do next.

Finally you say, "I can't stand not knowing what's down there and why that happened!"

Your friend seems to have recovered quickly because there's a twinkle in their eyes as they say, "We have to go back down!!"

You agree, so you both begin your decent again. You're not sure what to expect and more than a little afraid.

This time you're able to go to the spot much quicker than before. Once you find it, you stick your hand through. You slide your whole arm in and realize that there's no pain, or any feeling for that matter. You look at your friend and you both nod, so you make sure you'll fit through whatever weird portal this is by putting your hand above your head. You have to bend slightly, but you close your eyes and push through. Although "push" isn't exactly the word you would think of. It's more like glide through. There's a half a moment of the feeling of falling. A small cry escapes your lips as you hit the ground and sag into a crouch. You slowly open your eyes, to your surprise you are kneeling on a solid floor. You carefully let your breath out. Before going any further, you slip your hand through the wall and motion for your friend to come through. You see you friend's hand come through, then their shoulders, then the rest of them follow. The look on their face under different circumstances would have made you laugh, but laughing is the last thing on your mind right now. Your friend comes through closer to the floor and merely steps down slightly without losing their balance. They open their eyes and you both start to look around.

You are standing in what looks like a normal, medium-sized hallway. It's very bright and clean. At the end of it, it seems to turn. With shaky knees you start to walk. When you get down to the end, you find that it doesn't turn at all. Instead it ends in a small cubicle.

You are not sure what to do now. Your friend suggests exploring the wall with your hands.

"Maybe it'll be like the pool wall and will give way?"

So they start to the right and you start to the left. It doesn't take long to cover the whole room and when you are three feet apart from each other it happens again -whoosh- there goes your hands. Even though you were trying to be prepared for it, you still both jump a little. You remark that it's not like you hadn't done it before. This time though, your friend wants to go first. A few seconds later your friend is gone and it's your turn. With a pounding heart you follow.

Chapter 2

The Boy

Not realizing your eyes were shut, you open them and what you see is something you would have never expected.

"It's unbelievable!" you hear yourself say.

The floor is solid wood and shiny. To the left is a collection of the brightest neon beanbags. There is orange, blue, purple, yellow, red and green. Of all the things to be in an underground room behind a jellified wall, beanbags were not what you expected!

You momentarily forget to be anxious, and you smile. You look at your friend and they are smiling too, you just can't help it. To the right is a wood dining table that matches the floor and has three chairs around it. The rest of the room looks like a typical living room with a couch, chair, coffee table and a book shelf in the corner. You notice a cheery brightness present in the room. You look up to a very high ceiling, in the middle of which is a nice little chandelier. Your eyes travel to the far wall, where dozens of rainbows are cast from the chandelier.

You are enjoying the colors, when your friend suddenly asks, "What was that?!"

"What?" you reply.

"Listen."

Very faintly, like it's real far away, you hear what sounds like a small dog barking. You think that your ears are playing tricks on you. What would a dog be doing down here? Probably sleeping on the beanbags!

Slowly, your mind begins to function and you realize that somebody obviously must live here.

So you call out half embarrassed, "Hello? Anybody home? We don't mean any harm... anybody there?"

You here a dog barking, well just two barks, then a rhythmic clicking sound. Before you know it, a darling little dark colored Yorkshire Terrier comes through the wall on your right and trots towards you.

"Well hello there. Was that you making all that noise?"

The dog barks twice.

Your friend says, "She can't live here by herself."

She barks once.

While you are petting her, you find her tags, "Her name is Gumdrop."

She barks twice again.

"It sounds like she answering us." your friend says, "Let's test her, are you a good dog?" She barks twice.

"Are we dogs?" you ask with a grin.

She cooks her head to the side and barks once.

"Wow, she sure is a smart dog!"

Again, two barks.

You both laugh, especially since Gumdrop's mouth is hanging open, tongue lolling out, like she's laughing with you.

At first neither of you heard it, then he says it again, "Who are you? What do you want? Did *they* send you?"

You look at each other, startled and you say, "We don't mean any harm. We're sorry, but we just came in from the pool... it's okay we promise. Where are you anyway?"

"Are you sure they didn't send you?" the voice says. He sounded young and very concerned, but not panicked.

"No one sent us, we found this place by accident. We're just a couple kids that were swimming, that's all. ... You can trust us." you reply.

There is a slight pause, you both face the wall Gumdrop had come out of, having no idea what to expect.

A few seconds later, just like Gumdrop a young boy comes through the wall. He is about your age, sandy blonde hair, light green eyes, a healthy complexion, and medium built. He was one that could blend into a crowd if he had to, but far from ugly. He had on a pair of well worn blue jeans, a green tee shirt and sandals. He had a very intense expression on his face and was holding a small black object. It was wider than a TV remote control and almost as thick as an old walkman. It had a screen in the middle, surrounded by blinking lights and miniature toggle switches.

For a minute you just stare at him while he stares at the both of you. Then silence is broken by the clicking of Gumdrop's claws as she goes over to greet him.

Finally, after a good 45 seconds that seem like an eternity, he asks, "Are you sure it was just by accident that you found this place?"

"Yes we promise. No one sent us. We found that strange place in the pool wall by accident, really" you say trying to convince him.

As he bends down to stroke Gumdrop, you hear him mumble something about being careless about the pool entrance.

When he straightens up he turns to you and says, "Ok I believe you. What are your names? Do you go to school around here?"

You tell him your names as he walks over to shake your hand and say, "We go to school on the other side of town. We come to the college to swim because, - wait a minute, who are you? How did you get down here and have the ability to make walls jellified? And what is that thing in your hand? Is it a weapon?"

Somewhat startled at your last question he replies quickly that it's not a weapon, but that it's mostly the reason he's down here. He introduces himself as Steven Trevor Burton. After a pause he continues, "If I tell you anything more and you tell anyone else, we could all be in a bunch of trouble with some very powerful people."

You get the strong feeling that he needs to trust somebody, so you promise your silence. For the next fifteen minutes you learn briefly how and why it is he came to live underground.

His story began when he was three. His parents, Rebecca

and Steven Thomas Burton, disappeared in a boating accident at Lake Roberts. When he tells you this he gets a troubled expression on his face, and tells you that their bodies were never found. After the accident his father's best friend and partner, Ryan Perkins and his wife Vanessa, took Steven in as their own child. Then Ryan realized that Steven was without a doubt a genius, he encouraged Steven to pursue his education at his own speed. Because of this he was able to go through all his school, elementary, junior high and high school in a very small amount of time. He went through college in ten weeks! As Ryan supervised his schooling, he noticed Steven's interest and talent in the field of "Molecular Displacement," whatever that was, but you both just nod.

About six months ago it all started to get interesting when Steven made a breakthrough. He made it possible to pass through solid matter by rearranging it's molecules while still holding its original shape. That's where what he was holding in his hand came in. He called it a "Molecular Displacement Modulator." The Modulator was the finished result of his discovery.

A few weeks later after his breakthrough, the government found out what he had done and zeroed in on him and wanted to "buy it for further research." Ryan looked into it, calling on a few old friends and discovered that they were only interested in it for military purposes. They weren't giving them much choice in the matter and were starting to harass the family. So three months ago Ryan and Vanessa sat him down and explained to him what the government wanted to do. Steven did not agree with his invention being used by the military. So Steven dropped the project, and hid the files. They then decided that the Perkins were to go away. They said it was best that he didn't know where they were going to go at that time. They said that they loved him and would send for him as soon as they could. During the time they were gone he was to stay with his father's sister, Aunt Maggie. He told you she was his favorite aunt and that they were very close.

It was hard for the Perkins and Steven to say good-bye. They were the closest thing he had to parents, which he could remember. Ryan told him that if worst came to worst, he and Maggie had a plan, if Steven wanted to cooperate.

If the government kept hammering him, he was to fake his death and live in these rooms under the college that Gumdrop had discovered. When Ryan and Maggie saw this place they recognized that this would be safe for Steven to live here after he faked his death, until everything blew over.

While Steven was at Aunt Maggie's for the first month she taught him how to cook, clean, and generally care for himself. Then they had to go ahead and carry out the plan.

When he finished up the story he says, "There's more, but it would take too much time to tell you." He hesitates, "If you want to come back I can tell you a little more."

You and your friend look at each other, a little amazed and dazed at the whole thing. There's a small pause while you both think about what he told you.

"Well," you say slowly with a look at your friend, "I'd like to come back, um, it'd be nice to hear the rest." Your friend agrees.

You both nearly jump out of your skin when the clock on the wall chimes. You had no idea that much time had gone by. You remark that you have to get going.

Steven once again swears you both to secrecy. You promise and assure him he can trust you. There's an awkward silence as you all wonder how to say good-bye.

Steven ends up saying with a little smile, "Well, thank you for coming, look forward to seeing you again. If you want I can cook us lunch." You reply that sounds like a good idea.

You look around the room not sure where the "door" is. He realizes that you have no idea which way to go.

So he takes Gumdrop and holds her face in his hands while he says, "Pool, go to the pool." She barks twice and trots over to the wall that you now recognize as the wall you came through.

"Well, bye. We'll be back the day after tomorrow." You say as you and your friend turn to follow Gumdrop.

You go through the cubicle wall and down the hallway. When you come to the wall at the pool, Gumdrop looks up at you expectantly. You're both too lost in thought to realize that you're at your destination. She gives you a nudge with her cold nose and you jump. So you bid her good-bye, take a deep breath and slip through the wall.

You surface, followed closely by your friend. You are glad to find out that nobody has missed you. Thank goodness for distracted lifeguards. You get out and go to the locker-rooms. Not much is said as you both dry off, you are both too busy thinking.

While outside waiting for one of your parents, your friend asks, "Did that really happen?"

You reply with a shrug, and a bewildered look on your face. Until you are able to go back with your friend, as promised, your world seems unreal. You can only imagine what this visit will be like.

Chapter 3

The Lunch

You play around in the pool for a few minutes, and then go down to try to find the hole in the wall. While you are both underwater, you get a very strange feeling, like somebody made the water move behind you. You both turn to see Steven appear right beside you! Even though he is wearing a scuba tank and mask, you can see his wide smile. It scares you so bad, though, that you lose all your air. His smile quickly turns to concern when he sees his new friends are about to drown! He quickly gives you his air hose and you are able to gulp a couple breaths before shoving it urgently to your friend. You go through the wall, coughing, and wait for them to join you.

Once they join you, you exclaim between a few more coughs, "What was that?! Where did you come from? You scared us, almost literally to death!"

He apologizes and asks if you are both ok as he picks up a couple shirts for you to wear. Your friend replies that they're fine, but "Don't ever do that again!" He says he won't, at least not when you are still underwater.

As you are all walking back to the living area, he starts to get excited again. He asks if you realize what he was able to do. Both of you shrug, so he explains that this was an offshoot of the modulator project. He had been trying to transfer and reconstruct a person's molecules to underwater, and it had worked! He states that this had seemed like the next logical step in his work, and besides, he wanted to see if he could eventually go out to the lake where his parents disappeared and see if he could find some answers.

When you reach the living room he goes through the wall, he's still talking, but his voice becomes muffled so you can't quite hear what he asks you. There's a funny silence as he waits for you both to step through.

"Sorry," he says with a grin, "I guess I got too excited. Would you like something to drink?"

You both say yes and make a choice between the drinks he offers you.

"So let me get this straight, in plain English, you just beamed yourself into the pool?!" your friend asks.

After a pause, and a couple blinks he says, "Well.. yeah!"

He gestures for you to follow him, and you are not too surprised when he disappears through the wall to your right. You both hesitate for only half a second before following him. On the other side is a brightly lit, tiled, clean and well maintained room.

On the right is a mini kitchen with a stove, sink, refrigerator, a couple cabinets and some counter space. On the stove is a covered pot with something that smells wonderful. On the counter are three sandwiches, your favorite kind. You look at your friend surprised that he actually fixed a real meal. Without realizing it you had expected something like a T.V. dinner. You notice that he doesn't even have a microwave!

On the left is an area that has a work table. It has many wires, a couple of computer monitors, and they whole area looks like your basic laboratory. As you look around Steven is getting drinks and lunch ready. Your friend remarks that he's got a nice place. You notice that something is different, but you can't put your finger on what it is.

All three of you take the food back to the table which you hadn't noticed was set with three mats, and sit down. You are both surprised how good the food is and compliment Steven on the lunch. He says he wouldn't know how to boil an egg if it wasn't for his Aunt Maggie.

After a little small talk and some silence while you eat, your friend says, "So what else do you have to tell us Steven?"

He responds with a smile as he swallows his last bite. Before he can say anything though, you ask how he can stay down here without any contact from the outside world. He replies that he isn't "without contact from the outside world." His Aunt Maggie and him have a system to communicate.

You catch him glance at a wall and then at his watch before

he explains. He says that every day he and Maggie use Gumdrop as a carrier dog to take letters back and forth. They put letters in her collar and have what they call a 'drop spot,' where Maggie and Gumdrop meet every day at a certain time.

He explains to you that he tells her everything, if he's sick or whatever. So he never really has been alone. She's been a good aunt and always takes care of him. He's always known what's going on in the outside world. It dawns on you and your friend at the same time what was missing.

"Is that where Gumdrop is now?" Your friend asks.

Now you understand why it had seems like something was different, Gumdrop wasn't there.

He replies that he let her out before you had come and now he's starting to get worried, because she's usually back by now. Even when nature calls, she never takes this long. You like the dog too, and knowing Steven's situation, you start to get worried also.

Finally after a couple minutes, you hear a faint barking. It's a constant yapping that alarms Steven. You figure that it's not her usual pleasant greeting. As it gets louder, Steven's forehead becomes more and more creased.

Then Gumdrop comes bursting through the corner and into the room. Her claws make a lot of noise as she tries to put the brakes on, but the wood floor is making it very difficult. It's almost comical, her grand entrance, but Steven is by no means laughing. He bends down to pick her up, trying to calm her down.

Finally she settles down enough for Steven to ask her, "Are you ok?"

She barks twice.

"Were there any problems?"

Two barks.

"Is Aunt Maggie okay?"

Again she replies with two barks.

Steven feels around her collar for the letter from his aunt and pulls it out. You are not sure what to do as he reads the note, but as he does, his face turns almost totally pale.

You are afraid to ask, because you know you can't do anything anyway, but you say, "Steven, is something wrong?"

He tells you that Aunt Maggie says they should change the drop point because she's noticed some one hanging around the last few times. She says that it might be Professor Calhoun. She recognized him from seeing him around the college. After he tells you this he gets Gumdrops attention and asks her, "Were you followed?"

She barks twice.

"Did you lose them?" he asks, holding his breath.

She cocks her head to the side and after a short pause barks twice again. You didn't realize that you had been holding your breath too, until you let it out. You hear your friend let their breath out too.

Some of the tension visibly goes out of Steven's face. He takes a deep breath and says that he trusts Aunt Maggie to take care of any problems.

"Even if that means teaching Gumdrop a new drop spot," he says as he starts to clear the table.

You think you should help, so the three of you clean up and wash the dishes, talking the whole time. Doing chores had never been that enjoyable, and tell them that too.

After you are done, he goes the few feet to one of the monitors and starts mumbling to himself.

"What's the matter?" your friend asks.

"This dumb computer," he replies, more to himself than to the two of you, "Every so often the whole system goes ... haywire. It doesn't crash or anything, but it like blips or something. It's really annoying when it happens while I'm working."

While you and your friend remark on how strange that is, Gumdrop gets up from where she'd settled on the floor and trots purposefully through the wall into the living room. A second later she starts barking, you'd say it was to a rhythm if you didn't know better.

Wondering aloud what she wants Steven goes into the living room and of course you follow. Gumdrop is in the corner by the book shelf scratching while she continues to bark at the base of the corner. Steven says that she does that every now and then and doesn't know why. He goes over to her and tries to pull her away from the corner, but she fights him for a minute then gives up and starts licking his hands.

Your friend asks if there could be a connection to the computer blip and Gumdrop's strange actions. He picks her up and says that he never really thought about it.

"Might as well check it out with the computer." He says after a moment's thought.

So with both of your help he wheels in one of the desks, with the silent computer on top, into the living room. You ask him how he got all of this equipment down here.

He just smiles and says, "Secrecy. The dark is a wonderful thing."

With that comment he takes what looks to you like enhanced suction cups and puts four on the two walls that make up Gumdrop's favorite corner.

After a few adjustments he straightens up and turns on the computer. Once it boots up, you see data that looks like a foreign language to you, pop up every few seconds on the screen. While he is reading it over, you realize that you have to get back to the pool before somebody misses you.

When you tell Steven this, he turns around and requests very strongly that you come back. You promise that you will as soon as possible.

"It'll probably be in a couple days, we practically live at this pool during the summer." you friend says.

He replies that he is glad to hear that and looks forward to telling you what's up with the "mystery wall."

Then before he turns back to the display he says, "It's really nice to have friends to talk to again. Now I'm glad I was so careless with the hole in the wall!"

"Yeah we are too! This has got to be the best adventure we've ever had. And you can trust us too," you say.

With a final farewell, to both Steven and Gumdrop, you walk

through the wall and are surprised that you knew your way to the pool without thinking about it. As you slip through to the water outside, you think that you will never get used to the feeling of going from dry to wet in that unusual way.

Once again nobody missed you, thankfully. Your friend remarks that you have to be careful about that. It's so easy to get caught up in the events that happen underground and lose track of time.

While you are playing around in the pool, both of you decide to investigate this "Professor Calhoun" person.

"This should be interesting," you say, "I've always loved spying on people!"

Well, you were right about it being interesting.

Chapter 4

The Professor

When you ask one of your parents to use the college library, they seem a little confused, but when you add that you have some research to do, they say ok. You get an adrenaline rush when they start to ask what for, but as their first word is coming out their mouth, the phone rings. You are truly "saved by the bell!" After a little while you call your friend and make the arrangements to meet there.

Once you are standing inside the large library, you both wonder where to go from there. Then you get the idea to go to the yearbooks. Based on what Steven had told you about the timing of his parents disappearance, you get that year and two years before and after. As an afterthought you also grab the current yearbook. You divide them up and start looking for Calhoun, or anything else that is of interest.

At first you are both laughing at the old hairstyles and clothes, but after a little less than an hour, all the pages start to blur together and your friend mumbles that this is pointless. Just when they are about to suggest that you try something else, you see a picture in the yearbook two years before their disappearance with a group of people in it. Looking at the caption, which gives you the names of the people in the picture, two names jump out at you: V. Calhoun and S.T. Burton. "Oh wow!" you hear yourself say.

You show it to your friend, and you both stare at the picture. From what you can see, the quality of the picture isn't wonderful, Burton could be Steven, just a little older. He's a nice looking young man, in contrast with Calhoun, he looks like a guy you wouldn't want to meet in a back alley. He has sparse dirty looking hair that tries in vain to cover an oversized forehead, black rimmed glasses, a rather large nose hanging over a small crooked mouth. His chin is a little too sharply defined and it's easy to imagine his face in a constant sneer, as it is in the picture.

You're not surprised to find out that it is in the Science Department section. Reading the surrounding text, you find out that Burton was Calhoun's assistant. Your friend laughs when they read what Calhoun's first name is. "What?" you inquire.

They tell you that his name is Vernon. You smother a laugh while your friend asks, "What was his mother thinking?!"

After that short but funny break, you resume reading. Not much else is said about the two that interest you. You decide to go back over the next yearbook and see if there was anything you might have missed. In the Science section again, it informs you that Burton had his own lab and office. It made it sound like he left Calhoun and 'moved up in the world.'

Then you suggest looking for any articles that might say anything about how Burton got his own lab. So going to the computer, you find they have made it very easy for you. In the computer is a search engine, like on the Internet, so you just type in "S.T. Burton, Vernon Calhoun." Sure enough, it pulls up a short article about it. It says that the long time professor/assistant relationship of Burton and Calhoun was terminated because of "moral and creative differences." In the opinion of the writer, Burton did a good thing by "ditching" Calhoun. It sounded like Mr. Calhoun wasn't very well liked.

Now that your curiosities are going wild, your friend suggests looking in the directory to find out where and when this Professor works or teaches. 'I'd hate to have him as a teacher!' you think to yourself. The directory tells you where - Science and Technology building- and what -Physical Science- he teaches, but not when.

After much searching and asking a few questions without trying to be suspicious, you get your hands on a class schedule that gives you the time of his classes. You both know that you are going to try to see him. So without further ado, you head for the Science and Technology building.

As you approach the building, wondering how you are going to find his class room, a man comes out. The first thing you notice is that he's wearing a long-sleeve black shirt, blue jeans, and is carrying an umbrella, despite the cloudless sky.

The second thing you notice is his face, big nose, black rimmed glasses, and a nasty looking sneer. He hadn't noticed you yet, because his head was bent in thought. Your friend says, "Isn't that...oh man it is!"

If you didn't do something quickly, he would notice you and you didn't think the two of you could pass as students, at least not college students. Not only that, but you know both of your faces showed a combination of surprise and recognition, both of which would make him suspicious.

You and your friend look wildly around for something, anything, to dive behind. The only thing within reach is a couple small trees behind you. As you both dash for them you're sure he saw you.

Hiding behind your skimpy cover, you are afraid to breath, positive he will hear the pounding of your heart as he walks past. But nothing of the sort happens, and he walks by without even glancing your way. You get a clear view of his face and it's definitely Calhoun, older, uglier, and meaner looking. Once he's past you, relief and surprise are quickly followed by curiosity. You both know without a doubt that you are going to follow him. You wait until he is a safer distance away before venturing out of your hiding spot. You notice that his walk is very purposeful and determined.

He makes a few turns here and there. Because neither of you are very familiar with the college campus, you start to worry about being able to find your way back to the library. You continue following him at a careful distance though. He finally makes one final turn into an area that is a courtyard looking place. It's a landscaped circle with benches around the rim. In the middle, which is where Calhoun makes a beeline for, is a tree with bushes around the base. There are other various flowers and shrubs decorating the area too. Since there is lots of cover, you and your friend have no problem watching him without the threat of being seen.

After poking the ground at the base of the tree with his umbrella, he goes and sits down, staring at the tree. He doesn't have anything to read, he just sits there and stares intently at the ground. After a few minutes he gets up, walks around the tree and checks he watch every few seconds. He appears very impatient, like he's waiting for something. You give your friend a puzzled look.

They reply by whispering, "It looks like he's gone crazy!"

He goes back and sits down, all the while absorbed in watching the ground and bushes. At the end of about 20 minutes, he gets up, goes over to the base of the tree again and starts feeling the ground, literally on his hands and knees! You think for sure that he's lost his marbles, when the thought enters your head that this is the "drop site" where Aunt Maggie and Gumdrop meet. Right then, you can tell your friend thinks of the same thing, because they start hitting your arm and saying exactly what you had just thought of.

Before you can reply, Calhoun straightens up and stomps right towards you! You both scramble to get up and out of his way. You run around the corner and find a statue to hide behind. At least your current hiding place is better than the last one. He continues walking and the look on his face is the meanest you've ever seen. In comparison, the sneer from the yearbook was a smile!

After he disappears around a building, your heart starts to slow down. You both decide that you've had enough excitement for one day and head back to the library without any problems. While you wait around for one of your parents to pick you up, you start to get excited about telling Steven what you found out and saw.

Chapter 5

The Play Room

As it turns out, you're not able to go back to the pool for three days. You try not to show your excitement to your parents about telling Steven that they changed the drop spot just in time. Not to mention the fact that Calhoun and his father used to work together. You hope that it will help him figure out what happened, ultimately to his parents. Without realizing it, you suspect that they are still alive, but you're not sure why you think that.

You are afraid that your parents are starting to wonder why you want to go back to the college so bad. Even though there is a burning excitement inside, you do your best to act like it doesn't matter. When you talk to your friend though, you find out that they are going through the same thing. You both are thinking that it seems you'll never be able to go back!

Finally you get the okay to go back to the pool. You wish Steven had a phone so that you could tell him you're coming. As you walk inside your friend suggests getting "Aunt" Maggie's phone number in case either of you need it. As you get ready to go in the pool, you talk excitedly with your friend.

After a few tries and more than one spent lung full of air, you find the 'opening.' You both go through without any trouble and see the shirts Steven had loaned you on the floor, undisturbed.

While you walk down the hallway, your friend comments on how eerie it is down here. Except for the odd sound of your wet footsteps echoing on the clean floor, it is dead quiet.

Then you go through the wall that leads into Steven's home, he's not there to greet you. You don't think that is unusual, since he didn't know you were coming. But before going any further, you call out to him to let him know that you're here. When you don't hear an answer, you trade worried glances with your friend. As your do, you hear the sound of familiar barking, but it almost sounds like it's a mile away, or maybe through a tunnel.

You call out, "Gumdrop come here girl, come say hi."

At that, you see her trot through the wall opposite of you, which surprises you because you didn't know that was a soft wall. As you both lean down to pet her, your friend asks, "Wonder what's behind that wall, and where Steven is?" Then to Gumdrop they say, "Is Steven okay?"

Two barks.

Once again you call out to Steven.

Then, real faintly you hear, "I'm in here."

You and your friend say at the same time, "Where's here?!"

He instructs you to follow Gumdrop. So taking her face in your hands, you tell her to take you to Steven. When she turns back to the far wall she came from before, you're not surprised.

All of a sudden you get goose-bumps, or maybe it was a gut instinct saying something was not right. Hoping your friend didn't see it you quickly shake it off and go through the wall, without any more protest from your skin. On the other side is a very small room. It has a single bare light bulb hanging motionlessly and doing its best to cheer up the small area. It has a musty old smell to it and the light bulb throws shadows all around you. You can tell at a glance that Steven is not there.

You hear your friend let out an almost shaky sigh and sums it up in one word, "Spooky." Gumdrop barks at you a goes through the next wall in front of you. As you go through that wall you notice that it's a little harder to go through, it's not uncomfortable, but the smoothness is gone. It's not like gliding anymore, there's more of an effort to it.

The second room is slightly larger, but still very small. It also has the same type of bare bulb. The difference in this room is that the floor is covered with opened files, the first words that you think of are "organized mess." The biggest difference is that Steven is sitting in a corner, intently reading another file. Right underneath the file he is reading there is a red file that grabs your attention. When he finally looks up at the both of you, his eyes are red and bloodshot.

"Hi," he says awkwardly.

"Are you ok Steven?" your friend says with concern in their voice.

"I, ... yeah I'm ok. I... I've just been in here awhile," he stutters back.

"What happened, what is all this?" you ask him.

Barely above a whisper he replies, "It's all my father's work. Every paper, every note... everything he ever worked on! I've gone through most of it already, but still have a little more to cover."

"You look like you could use a break," your friend says, "How about taking a rest for a minute?" He blinks a couple times, looks back at the file he was reading and then at the red file. "I guess that would be a good idea, I've been in here for, well I don't really know how long. It's been quite awhile this time."

As you help him up, he seems a little wobbly, but able to walk after a second. You all go back through both walls, and when you get back into the living room, you realize that you were quite uncomfortable in there. It reminded you too much of a tomb.

Before he washes his face and gets a drink, he gives you a note and mumbles that you need to read it. You start to read it out loud to your friend...

"My Dear Steven, I thought you needed a little more background as to why we had to change the drop site, I owe you that much.

The reason I recognized the man hanging around the drop site was because he is Professor Calhoun. He used to work with your dad at the university many years ago. He was his boss, and after awhile the project that your father was working on came to the attention of the government. Calhoun wanted to okay the project being turned over to the government, he used the excuse that he had no choice. But your father suspected that he wasn't telling the whole story and was offered a large amount of money, which he would have kept for himself of course. With a little investigation, he found out that's exactly what Calhoun was going to do.

But your dad wasn't going to allow the government take advantage of his project and cause a lot of damage. So he took his work elsewhere, having obtained a lab of his own, thanks to a timely promotion."

You both stop there and look at each other with the realization that this was exactly what you had found out at the library. But nothing could have prepared you for what you were about to read. It is something you never would have thought of.

Maggie continues, "The reason there was a problem was because Professor Calhoun recognized Gumdrop. Brace yourself Steven, what I'm about to tell you will come as a shock: Gumdrop was your father's dog."

When your read that, both of you let out an unconscious, "Whoa!"

In fact you scare each other when it escapes your lips. Right at that moment Steven comes from the kitchen patting his face with a towel.

"Pretty amazing isn't it!? I still can't wrap my mind around the fact that Gumdrop was my dad's dog!"

As he says this he leans over to pet her. You can tell there is a new light in his eyes looking at her. In a way, you could understand what he was thinking, she was something passed on from a long lost father. Little did you know that his father had passed on much more than just a cute little pet and friend.

Your friend breaks the silence and asks if Steven's handling all this okay. He states that it's interesting to say the least and motions for you to sit down. Then he proceeds to explain what had happened. He had been checking out the "mystery wall" and discovered that there was a regular pulse signal coming from it. He says that the computer's blips and Gumdrops odd behavior had only started a couple days ago, so he didn't think that the signal had been emitting from the wall for very long.

In order to get through the first wall, he said he had use the signal to calibrate the modulator to a slightly different frequency. Obviously, there was nothing in the first room that would make the signal, so he tried to go through the next wall. He stated that it was harder to calibrate and took him longer to figure out how to fine tune the modulator. In the second room, once he saw all the files, he had to read them.

He still looks a little dazed when he says, "I just can't believe that my dad and I both worked in Molecular Biology! Ryan must have known, but he never told me. He never even pushed me into this field, just encouraged me in whatever direction I liked the most." After this he is quiet for a moment.

"I have to get back to reading those last two files. Would you mind waiting? I have something I've wanted to show you anyway. It'll keep you busy for awhile." He says with the beginnings of a smile.

He gets up and leads you to the wall opposite the 'kitchen.' You follow him through it, almost laughing that it's beginning to feel normal to walk through walls! On the other side it is mostly dark, with a small light fixture right beside you on the wall.

Steven says, "I created this for the times when I need a break. I've been dying to show it to somebody. I wish I could stay, but I need to get back to those files. Have fun!"

As he leaves he reaches over and flips up a light switch and what you see is, like everything else here, amazing. You thought that you'd be prepared for anything, your mind has already been numbed by what you've seen and heard in the last week.

Your friend let's out another, "Whoa!"

The room has a very high ceiling, about 30 feet or more, and the whole room is very large. It looks like a play area. The first thing that you notice is a large metal thing. It is about 20 feet high and has a ladder going up to a platform. There are some rope looking things hanging down. Right below it is a big square about 10 by 10 feet. Looking around the rest of the room you see a padded floor, like for gymnastics, rings, and a huge trampoline with a hanging harness.

Turning your attention back at the large metal contraption, you both walk over to the square which is about 4 feet above the ground, and look at what's inside it. The first thing that comes to your mind to describe it is Jell-O, but it's not shiny. It's grass green in color, looks spongy and it absorbs the light. You poke your finger in it first and it gives way. Your friend puts their hand in and it looks like something pushes it back out again.

"Oh man, you've got to try this!" They exclaim.

When you do, it really feels like there's a force shoving your hand back up. You even push your arm in up to the elbow, and it just pushes it out all the harder.

"It's like perpetual motion!" You say. You both walk around to the 'front' of the square so that you're facing the ladder that goes up to the platform. Your friend and you both look up, and at the same time it hits you that this is bungee jumping in the safest way possible. You tell your friend that you've always wanted to bungee jump.

You both agree that this is a now or never situation and should go for it. After all, what if something happens and you don't have this chance again?! You tell your friend that they better come up with you and they say "After you!"

So with a pounding heart you climb up to the platform and immediately realize that it's a little higher than you thought. The thought of the stuff underneath is a small comfort. Your friend insists that you go first, since 'you were the one who always wanted to bungee jump!' You pull the harness up and figure out how it goes on. It's practically a full body harness, going up around your shoulders, down to your waist and through your legs. At least you don't have to worry about dislocating anything.

Once you get it on, you step to the edge and start to turn to your friend and say "I don't know about this."

But before you can finish the sentence, your friend pushes you off!

You fall, screaming the whole way that you now hate your

friend! When you hit the landing area, you go in up to your thighs and spring back out. You fly all the way back up to the platform.

It's funny because, your eyes are about level with your friends knees. They, needless to say, are laughing their head off and by the time you hit the pad again, you're laughing too. It's the strangest sensation, to be hurled through the air by that green goop! After a few bounces, you're ready to start trying a few tricks. That's the fun part, spinning around in somersaults, twists and whatever other crazy things your body decides to do. After a couple minutes, you begin to wonder how to stop, not that you want to.

But eventually you will need to, besides your friend has to try it too! Your friend the whole while is laughing at your distorted "tricks."

You yell if they know how to stop this thing. After a few unlikely suggestions, you decide to sit when you hit. When you do that the bouncing motion isn't nearly as strong and you don't go down half as deep. With a few bounces with your legs out in front of you, you come to a complete stop and roll off the square. It's a little hard to do, with the harness still attached, but you manage to get it off and get back to solid ground without too much hassle.

You start to tell your friend that they have to try it, but they are already pulling the harness back up to the platform. You decide to stay on the ground for now and watch from here. It takes a minute for them to get the harness on. Once they do, they hesitate only a second before leaping off the platform. You had never wished for a video camera more than at that moment. The look on their face as they fall is priceless! They, like you did, fall into the goop up to their thighs. Of course you're laughing at both their face and the noises coming out of their mouth. Of course they go through all the distorted "tricks" that you did.

As the height of the jumps gets lower and lower, you start looking around at what else is in the room and are starting to play around on the padded floor. Your friend gets off and joins you right as Steven comes bursting through the wall carrying the red file.

"You guys won't believe what I found!!!

Chapter 6

The Red File

You get a surge of adrenalin that pumps through your body. You aren't given much of a chance to recover though. Steven is already heading back through the wall yelling for you both to follow him.

As you all go back through the two walls he's babbling on about "disruption chambers" & "molecular suspension." You are, of course, totally lost, but he doesn't seem to notice.

Once you get to the second room, your friend interrupts and asks him the obvious question that was on your mind too, "What are you talking about?!"

He takes a deep breath and says that the last file, the red one, is the key to bringing his parents back. The look of total confusion on your faces contrasts with the look of sheer joy and excitement on Steven's face. He says patiently that his parents aren't dead and that with the help of this red file, he can bring them back.

"You keep using that phrase," you say, "What do you mean "bring them back?"" He's too busy making sure the modulator has the right frequency to answer right away, but when he finally looks up, he says, "I'm going to bring them back from nowhere."

With that puzzling answer hanging in the air, he continues to work on the modulator.

Just when you begin to think that you can't take the stifling room, and the silence, he looks up quickly and says, "Ok it's definitely the right frequency, let's go."

The calmness in his voice surprises, and comforts you to a degree. He disappears through the wall and for once your friend and you aren't quite sure that you want to follow. It's just that creeping feeling again. But Steven is your friend, and if his parents are alive, then you want to be there when they "come back." Whatever that means.

After a deep breath, you tell your friend that you'll go through. This wall is the hardest you've been through yet.

Steven is already working at a console, with a light behind him on the wall. It shines into the room just barely enough for you to see a chamber in the center. It has a metal band around the middle, with a slowly blinking red light. It's about seven feet tall and it looks like you could barely wrap your arms around the front of it, if you tried. Even though the front of it is made of glass, you can't make out anything inside. It looks like a very slowly moving light bluish cloud.

Your friend is taking this in beside you. After a few moments, you look over at Steven, he is still busy consulting the red file, setting dials and typing on the very old dust covered keyboard at the console to your left. He's mumbling slightly, words you've never even heard before.

Besides the sound of him working, you notice a faint hum, coming from the chamber. Your friend and you are both silent, afraid that if you spoke you'd wake up from this unbelievable dream.

All of a sudden Steven straightens up saying, "Ok... here we go..." He types in a final command, hits the enter key and focuses his attention on the chamber. Following his gaze, you turn to look at the chamber. The little blinking red light changes to solid yellow and slowly the fog inside starts to swirl. Unable to take your eyes off of the turning mass, you watch as it starts to disappear, melting away from the top.

For about a foot there is nothing. Then your heart nearly jumps out of your chest when what appears to be the top of a head comes into view! You almost let out a yelp, but for some reason your body and mind seem to be disconnected. Your brain knew to expect to see something like that, but actually taking it in with your eyes is totally different. For a moment you wonder if you are dreaming again. All of this goes through your head in the fraction of a second. As the fog continues it's downward spiral, more of the face comes into view. You can tell it's a man, in fact he looks a lot like Steven. Perhaps it'd be more accurate to say Steven looked a lot like him. An odd thing is that his hair is wet. As the fog continues down, the rest of him comes into view. Like his head, the rest of him is sopping wet. His eyes are closed and he's wearing a polo shirt and tan shorts. It seems to take forever for the fog to clear completely. When it is about at his knees you tear your eyes away to look at Steven. He has a mixture of emotions on his face that you can't exactly identify. One that you can identify is impatience. You and your friend are equally speechless.

Once the fog clears completely, the yellow light starts to blink and there is a hissing noise from the rear of the chamber. Finally the light stops blinking and turns to green. Steven goes over to the chamber, he looks like he's on auto pilot. As he does, a light comes on inside the chamber slowly getting brighter. He reaches out and touches the only button on the metal band. The experience of seeing the light brighten, and knowing what was about to happen, takes the breath from your chest. The door opens and what you hear sounds like air escaping from a balloon, but without the squeak. The man inside slowly opens his eyes and looks around without moving his head. Steven is stock still and speechless. The man tilts his head to one side, then the other, seemingly testing his ability to move. You can see a few of his other muscles tighten and loosen, till he squints into the void of the open door.

"Steven?" It was both a question and a statement. He had to have known that his son was the only one who could bring him back.

Steven stepped a little closer to the chamber and more into the light. The look on the man's face was like nothing you had ever seen.

"Dad!" That was the only word he could get out. You could only imagine the emotions inside Steven now. His dad takes a shaky step to the edge of the chamber and holds out his arms, to his slightly sobbing boy. What a reunion! You almost feel nosy watching this scene before you.

Gumdrop though, wouldn't be forgotten and as Steven and his dad come more out of the chamber, she trots over to them. She barks in short yips and her whole body is shaking from the vigorous movement of her hind end.

"Gumdrop!!!" Steven Sr. says, "I'm so glad to see you!"

He leans down to pet her and she jumps into his arms, licking any patch of skin she can get her tongue on. It's such a sweet little meeting, long lost owner with loyal dog.

Steven Jr. is still stunned. He looks over at you and your friend with a tear of joy in his eyes, "Can you believe this?!"

You can't really think of anything else to do but smile broadly. It's obvious that Steven Sr. is very surprised to see other people on this amazing occasion. A little timidly you walk over, followed closely by your friend, and extend your hand, "Hi." is what you manage to say in this semi-awkward situation. Steven blinks a few times and stuttering, introduces you.

Then he says, "This is my *dad!*"

Chapter 7

The Problem

He looks like he still hasn't wrapped his mind around the fact.

"I know Steven! It's great!" you reply.

Steven Jr. is hugging his dad like he's afraid that he'll disappear back into the void he came from, but all of a sudden he asks, "Dad, where's Mom?!"

The look on Steven Sr. face is one of bad news.

"Son, she was... sick before. She had cancer. We suspended her in another chamber, but if there isn't a cure, she won't have very long to live."

Steven's head drops as he breaths out.

"There's no cure Dad."

"I was afraid of that. But she made me promise that even if there wasn't a cure that I'd bring her back anyway. She really wanted to see you," he replies.

Another tear slides down Steven's cheek, one of sadness, not of joy.

"Well, where is she?"

"She's in the next room."

His dad says as he walks towards the console and pulls out what looks like another modulator.

"We need to use this one to get to her."

The new, or rather old, one is bigger and has a few more switches on it. As he aims it at the far wall, Steven's head is bent in thought. You can tell that his mind is working overtime and you are about to ask him what he's thinking when the far wall begins to bulge. You've never seen a wall converted before and it's something you'll never forget. It ripples out from where the modulator is pointed at it, creating a pebble in the pond effect. It looks like it phases clear for a second then it reforms back to the appearance of a normal wall. Of course, you know that it is anything but a "normal" wall now. Steven Sr. motions for his son to go through, but Steven is too busy thinking.

"Dad" he says, "I'm not totally familiar with the medical field, but do you think it's possible to maybe.... filter out the cancerous cells using the modulators? I've had some success in separating different cells. I had to stop that field of research because it took too much power, but what do you think?"

It's so odd to see the look on Steven Sr.'s face because it's the same look that you've seen on your new friend's face many times.

As he thinks, he blinks slowly. "Son, I think that might work..."

Then he goes off into a long discussion with Steven about the technical side of the idea. Just when you start to think maybe you should get going, they suddenly stop talking and look at each other, "Then let's do it!" Steven Sr. says.

"What exactly are you going to do?" your friend asks.

With a slight smile Steven says, "We're going to save my mom! It's a long shot, but it's all we have."

"Is there anything we can do?" you say.

"Not at the moment, but I would really like you to stay." So with nothing to do but watch father and son work, you both stand there, feeling useless. They disappear through the wall so you and your friend follow without hesitation. The smoothness is back, it takes no effort whatsoever to make it through this wall. On the other side, it's a mirror image of the room you just came from, same console, one chamber, etc.

Steven goes right over to the console and begins the process of bringing his mom back. His dad, meanwhile, is still working on both of the modulators with Gumdrop looking up at him. Soon, the chamber draws your attention, the fog is beginning it's downward spiral. It surprises you that she's rather pretty, in spite of the pale tone to her face. Steven disappears for a moment and comes back with a blanket for her. When Steven Sr. presses the button to open the door, you can tell by the look on his face that he's worried.

As she is helped down the step, Steven puts the blanket around her and hugs her silently. After a few moments of emotional silence, they explain their idea to her. It involves going back into the chamber, and she isn't too happy about that.

Steven suggests that we all go back to the living room so he and his dad can work out the details.

On the way back through the three rooms, they introduce you and your friend. It's sad, but by the time you all reach the living room, she is already out of breath and wanting to sit down.

She laughs a little as she sits and says, "It feels like I haven't sat down in years!" You can't help but chuckle, in reality, she hasn't. While Steven and his dad disappear into the lab, you sit and visit with Rebecca Burton. She's very nice and enjoys hearing about your adventures with her son during the past weeks.

After a short time, father and son rejoin the three of you and say they are ready to begin preparing. They ask for your help in disconnecting all the power supplies to the computers from the lab and explain that they're going to have to funnel all the power they have into the console through the modulators.

"It'll probably burn them out, but it'll be worth it, if it works." Steven Sr. says.

Your friend asks why it wouldn't work and Steven says, "If there's not enough power, we could lose hold on her cellular signature and not be able to bring her back... ever. But I'm pretty sure it'll work."

"So she could be lost for good then?" your friend asks.

"Yeah, but I can't think about that, I have to think it'll work."

"Of course it will, with two geniuses I'm sure you can figure it out!" you say with confidence.

As you help carry the cables and extension cords back to the fourth room, you discover that they won't reach. They will reach the third room though, and they have to spend some time transferring data from one console to another.

You and your friend are happy to help, but the time factor is starting to make you uneasy. It's been far too long now. Your parents will start getting worried soon... but neither of you want to leave. 'Surely they'll understand,' you reason to yourself, your friend thinking the same thing.

Once they get everything set up, you all go back to get Rebecca. When you all make it back to the third room, she hugs her husband and her son, "If this doesn't work, I don't want you two blaming yourselves, understand? You will have done everything humanly possible."

They agree and help her back into the damp chamber. "I love you" both Stevens say at the same time.

Taking a deep breath Steven goes over to the console, his dad right behind him. All the power sources had been concentrated into one cable, which had been plugged in to one end of the modulators.

Using an adaptor, they had hooked both modulators together. They, in turn, were plugged into the console. They look at each other, nod and start typing, flipping switches and adjusting dials.

Not sure what to expect, you and your friend turn, once again, to the chamber. Surprisingly, the only thing that happens is the light inside goes bright and the light on the band around the chamber goes to a solid yellow. She just stands there, bravely, knowing that at any moment she could break into a zillion pieces and never see her family again. On the other hand, without this risk, she'd be leaving them soon enough. You don't know how she looks so calm and collected. Pretty soon the light dies down and the green light comes on again.

"We did it, son." Steven Sr. says with relief in his voice.

You all go over to the chamber and watch as she steps out shakily.

"That was an experience I'll never forget!"

She is still weak and has to sit down, after hugging everyone.

"I'm so proud of you two! I used to call them my Dynamic Duo, they are more so now than ever!"

"We're so glad that you're ok, Mrs. Burton!" your friend says, "But if we don't leave very soon our parents are going to be worried." They agree and ask you to come back the following Wednesday, it being Saturday today. Following a hasty but heartfelt goodbye to everyone, including Gumdrop, you and your friend practically run back to the pool. You both shoot to the surface as quickly as possible and get out without trying to attract attention. You walk hurriedly to the locker rooms, drying off and changing in record time. As you almost run down the long hallway to the door you see your mom's car there and she is just starting to get out. You and your friend look at each other and sprint for the door before she gets to it and run through it apologizing thoroughly.

You get nothing more than the remark "I was starting to worry about you two," and a scolding look. After another apology and a few minutes in the car, you both start to breathe easier. After your friend is dropped off you start to think about how glad you are that you have someone to worry about you. Lots of kids don't.

Chapter 8

The End, Or Is It?

As the next few days go by uneventfully, you are really happy for Steven and his reunited family. It surprises you greatly though, on Monday you get a phone call from someone you would have never guessed. Your mom answers the phone and tells you it's for you.

Somewhat puzzled you pick it up, "Hello?"

"Hello, this is Aunt Maggie, would you like to join me for a swim?"

Your insides seem to go on pause for a second, your heart stops and your lungs forget how to breath.

"Of course, when?" you respond after you collect yourself.

"Tomorrow at 1:30. Bring your friend."

"Thank you, see you then."

Your mom is a little curious and asks who it was. Thinking

quickly you answer truthfully, "It's a friend I made at the college. They asked if I could go swimming tomorrow around 1:30, is that ok?"

"I suppose, as long as your chores are done."

Breathing a sigh of relief you call your friend as soon as you can and tell them what happened. They get permission too and you both can hardly wait till the next day.

When it finally comes, you go directly to the 'hole' in the pool and slip through. Walking down the hallway once again, you think about how much has happened since the first time you dared to walk down this hallway and into Steven's life.

Before walking through the living room wall you call out to make sure they're there and expecting you. They immediately say come in. It's quite a contrast to what you were expecting. It looks like they're in the middle of moving, as there are boxes stacked all along the wall. The coffee table, bookshelf and dining table are nowhere to be seen. The only thing unaffected is the chair and couch. There, on the couch, is where you see the Burtons. It's quite a sweet sight, actually, to see the three of them sitting together. Steven looks more like a son now, rather than a mini-scientist. Sitting in the chair is a tall, slender lady with gray streaked black hair. Even if you didn't know who this was, it would be easy to tell that she was related to Steven. She stands up when you enter the room and says hello.

"Hello Aunt Maggie," your friend says with a grin on their face.

After formal introductions, they explain the reason why they invited you as soon as possible.

"We couldn't wait the extra day," Steven Sr. starts out, "We have reason to believe that Calhoun is up to his old tricks and is very close to discovering our secret. That of course is unacceptable. As a solution, we've decided to leave here and bury the evidence, so to speak."

"We're going to implode the whole place so Calhoun can't ever prove anything." Steven puts in.

"What does imploding do?" your friend asks.

"You know how an explosion blows up or out?" Steven asks and you both nod, "Well an implosion collapses back onto itself."

"Where will you go?" you ask.

They tell you that the Perkins have a place for them up north in Wyoming. When the Perkins left Steven, that's where they went and they have been there since then. Through Maggie they've already contacted them and will be leaving tomorrow.

The news makes you happy that everyone will get to see each other again, but at the same time, it means you're losing your new friends.

"You probably won't be coming back then?" you ask even though you already know the answer.

"No, we won't," Steven Sr. says, "but that doesn't mean that you can't come and visit us. We'd be happy to have you any time you're up that way."

"We'd have to sell our parents on the idea," your friend points out.

Rebecca suggests that you don't tell your parents anything

about what's happened just yet, "Perhaps it'll be more believable coming from us."

You and your friend quickly agree.

Before all that will happen, they have a favor to ask of you, "Would you mind checking up on Calhoun to see what he's doing?" Steven requests, "One of us would do it, but he knows all of our faces."

You willingly agree to help, always up for another adventure. After a few more minutes of chatting about their move, you realize that it's time to get going. You get Maggie's phone number and agree to call her with your report on Calhoun. You say your goodbyes and actually get to swim for a little while before it's time for your parent to come.

The next day you and your friend arrange to get dropped off at the library again. Once you are sure your parents are out of sight, you head straight for Calhoun's building. Walking by his classroom produces nothing, he's not there. You know he has to have an office around here, so you check the information board and find out where it is. Walking by there without looking suspicious is a little harder, but you give it a shot anyway. Your pounding heart has nothing to be afraid of though, because he's not there either.

Somewhat stumped you and your friend walk back through the building. Not knowing where to look now you sit on the steps outside. Before long your friend has the idea to check that courtyard place you followed him to last time. Having no other ideas, you decide to proceed.

It's a little difficult to find it again, but after some wandering around you come upon it rather suddenly. There in the middle of the courtyard is Professor Calhoun himself. He has a shovel in his hand and is digging around the base of the tree that stands in the middle of the area. Fortunately, he's too busy with what he's doing to notice the two kids standing there staring at him. After recovering from the shock of seeing him almost right in front of you, you both dive behind a bush that has a good view of Calhoun. Before long, his shovel appears to slip into the ground half way. Calhoun stops, and carefully puts his hand through the "solid" earth. It's strange to see the look of joy on his face. It doesn't look like it's an emotion he often shows. You trade worried glances with your friend. As you do, Calhoun goes back to shoveling around what you know is the old drop spot.

All of a sudden you feel a low rumbling. Your first thought is an earthquake, but the buildings are not moving. You can just feel it under your feet. Your attention is drawn back to Calhoun when he starts muttering "No, no, no!" It starts out softly at first but then gets louder.

"NO!" He yells, he uselessly pokes the ground with the shovel again. You both know that the Burton's secret is now safe from Calhoun. The implosion was a success. Leaving him to his disappointment, you and your friend sneak away quietly. When you get back home, you call Maggie and tell her what happened. She asks to talk to one of your parents and you sit there trying to hear both sides of the conversation they are having. The call lasts a while and you're curious to hear what they're going to say about what's happened.

When your parent hang up the phone, they look more than a little surprised.

"You certainly have had a busy summer! From everything Maggie has told me, the Burtons sound like nice people, I'm glad you were able to help them out. Next time you go on a little adventure like that, though, let me in on it." They say with a sideways glance, "Oh, and they invited us up to Wyoming this winter break to meet them. We'll have to see about that. Although, I've always wanted to visit Wyoming." With a smile, they walk out the room.

Hmm, wonder what adventures there are to be had up north?